ROBERT WELBER

The Train

Illustrated by Deborah Ray

Pantheon Books

Dolores—I love you

Text Copyright © 1972 by Robert Welber
Illustrations Copyright © 1972 by Deborah Ray

All rights reserved under International and Pan-American Copyright Conventions. Published in the United States by Pantheon Books, a division of Random House, Inc., and simultaneously in Canada by Random House of Canada Limited, Toronto.

Library of Congress Cataloging in Publication Data

Welber, Robert. *The Train.*

Summary: A little girl tries to conquer her fear of the grassy meadow between the house and the train tracks.
I. Ray, Deborah, illus.   II. Title.
PZ7.W4482Tr [E] 72-461
ISBN 0-394-82430-X ISBN 0-394-92430-4 (lib. bdg.)

Manufactured in the United States of America

CL

I want to watch the trains go by,"
Elizabeth said to her father.

"Go on," he said.

"I can't go by myself," she said.

"Sure you can. It's just across the
meadow."

"I'm afraid to go alone," Elizabeth
said.

"What are you afraid of," her father said. "It's just a walk across a field. There is a fence in front of the track."

"I want you to go with me."

"I can't go with you now. I have to work. Maybe this afternoon I can go. Perhaps your mother can take you now."

Elizabeth made a face at her father and walked out of his study. She heard him begin to type. She sat on the window seat at the bottom of the stairs and looked out. She saw the long meadow with the tall summer grass, almost as tall as she was now, and at the very end was the high fence. She could barely see the fence.

She couldn't go alone. They were

4

wrong. Who knew what was waiting
in the grass?

But soon the noon train would be
going by.

She went to find her mother. Her mother was writing music.

"I want to watch the trains go by," Elizabeth said to her mother.

"Go on," her mother said.

"I can't go by myself," she answered.

"Yes you can, Elizabeth. There's nothing to be afraid of, child. Just walk slowly across the meadow and stand by the fence."

"I'm afraid to go alone."

"Why?" her mother asked.

"There are things in the grass," Elizabeth said.

"Who told you?"

"Tony."

"Tony had no right to tell you that. It isn't true," her mother said. "There's nothing there that could hurt you. No thing. I can't go now, honey. Maybe later on. Maybe Tony will take you, or Georgie. Ask your sister Georgie."

"Me go too," Amy said from behind her mother.

"No you stay with me, Amy. Our song is almost finished."

Elizabeth looked sad but she did not cry.

Elizabeth found Georgie outside the barn. Georgie was sitting on an old tire, painting a doll.

"Georgie, will you take me to see the noon train go by? Please, Georgie! I can't go by myself. Please! Please!"

"I can't now, Lizzie. I'm painting Amy's doll for her. She keeps saying she wants a blue doll. It's really not as far as it looks. Tony was just trying to scare you, Lizzie. Go on. You can do it. I'll watch you from here."

"I can't, Georgie, I can't."

And Elizabeth began to cry. She sat down on the ground and cried.

Georgie put the doll down carefully and went over to her sister. She patted her head.

"Maybe I can go this afternoon," she told Elizabeth. "I don't know." But Elizabeth didn't stop crying.

Suddenly across the field came the boom of the diesel engine's horn.

10

Boom Boom B-boom.

They both looked up and saw the diesel engine pulling a long freight train across the countryside. The grass was too tall and the train too far away to see it well.

Elizabeth put her head in her arms, her hands over her ears. Georgie went back to painting the doll.

Elizabeth was playing in her room when the afternoon train went by. She heard the horn blowing across the meadow. She put her hands over her ears.

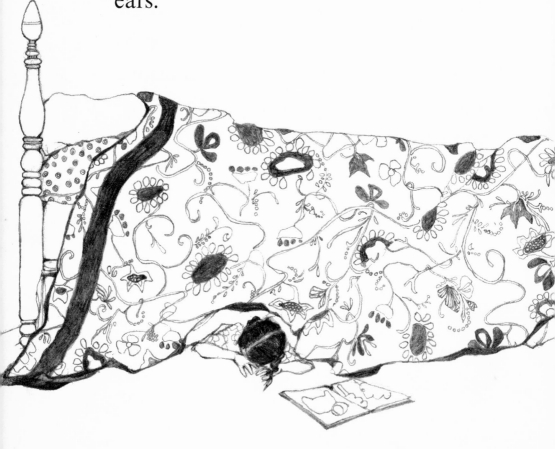

They all had forgotten her.

They all had taken her across the meadow to see the train go by many times, at different times. But the more she went the more she wanted to go. She wanted to see all the trains go by every day. Yes, watch the morning train go by, the noon train, the afternoon train, the evening train.

They were at dinner when the evening train went by. She stopped eating her soup and put her hands over her ears.

"Lizzie's scaredy-cat, scaredy-bat, scaredy-scaredy-scaredy-fat."

"Tony," his mother said sternly. "You stop teasing your sister this instant. There's nothing wrong in being afraid. Everyone is afraid

sometimes. When Elizabeth is ready she will go by herself."

"You used to want a light on all the time when you went to sleep, didn't you, Tony?" his father asked.

"Yes," Tony said quietly. "But I don't need it anymore."

"No you don't," his father said.

"Remember when we first came how afraid I was to go in the barn?" Georgie said and laughed. Everyone giggled. Even Elizabeth looked over at Georgie and smiled.

"Well, you might not have known it, but when we first came I was afraid to go down to the basement," her mother said.

Elizabeth put her spoon down in her soup and stared at her mother.

"The basement isn't scary," Elizabeth said. "Why, Mother?"

"We always lived in the city and I didn't know what would be in a country basement," her mother said.

"But there's nothing down there but

16

canned goods and stuff," Elizabeth said.

"I know, Elizabeth," her mother said.

"Your mother thought animals might be living there," her father said, and he smiled at her mother.

"Well, not exactly. Anyway, the point is, Elizabeth, whatever was there was worse in my mind than it really was," her mother said.

"How did you ever go down there?" Elizabeth asked slowly.

"She had courage," her father said.

"Lizzie has no courage, no tourage, no purage."

"Tony. Stop that. Maybe it was courage," her mother said. "Courage is doing something you're afraid of doing and doing it anyway."

All the next day Elizabeth sat in the hot sun staring across the field at the fence and the railroad track beyond.

She heard the morning train go by and the noon train and the afternoon train. She sat quietly listening. No one disturbed her or came near her all day.

At dinner she stopped eating when the evening train came by. Her face was tight and listening.

"Tony," Elizabeth asked later, "what do you think is in the meadow?"

"Nothing, Elizabeth," Tony said. "I was just teasing you."

"That's not true," Elizabeth said. "Mother told you to say that. Tony, what is in the meadow? You've been there. Tell me."

Tony was silent. Everyone was silent. Elizabeth looked slowly at all of them.

"There *are* some things there," she said. "Some things no one can see. There was no wind but the grass was moving. I saw it. I watched all day."

"Those are animals that make their home there, Elizabeth. But if you do not hurt them they will leave you alone," her father said. "You are much bigger than all of them. They'll probably be afraid of you."

Elizabeth sighed, half cry, half desperation.

"I want to see the trains go by," she whispered to herself.

But she was afraid.

She sat in the window seat all the next day, staring across the meadow, waiting for the trains to go by. She was alone. Tony was visiting a friend. Georgie had gone to the city.

Just before noon her mother came with Amy in her arms.

"Come on, Elizabeth. I'll take you across the meadow. We'll go together."

"No," Elizabeth said. "If I go, I'm going to go by myself."

Her mother was silent. Then she leaned over and gave Elizabeth a kiss and went on upstairs.

She heard her mother trying to put Amy to sleep. Amy wasn't sleepy. Elizabeth sat in the window seat the whole long day.

22

She heard Tony come in and throw his stuff on the floor. Her mother made him take it to his room. He passed her on the staircase but didn't speak.

She heard Georgie come into the kitchen and Amy run to her. Then they went to Amy's room. They passed her on the staircase but they didn't speak to her. Her mother and father were talking low in the kitchen.

She was all alone, all alone, she

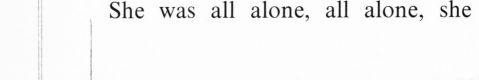

thought, and she stared at the meadow in the twilight.

"Lizzie." It was Tony standing behind her. She didn't turn around.

"Lizzie," he said, "there's nothing to be afraid of, really. I'll take you over."

"No," Elizabeth said. "I'll go by myself."

"Don't be afraid, Lizzie. There's nothing to hurt you."

"Then why did you say there was?" she asked.

"I was teasing you," Tony said.

She turned to look at him. He was tall above her in the shadowy light.

"Tony—" she began, but their mother called them in to dinner. They both walked in silently and sat down.

That night in bed she decided she would go across the meadow the next morning, early in the morning before anyone was up. She would see the early-morning train go by.

She would think about the train as she crossed the meadow and nothing else. She would walk firmly and steadily and that would be that.

She hugged her pillow, excited, and she was afraid. She knew Tony was telling the truth now, they all were. She had crossed the meadow so many times with the others. It would be all right.

But she was afraid.

She dressed quickly before the sun came up. Everyone else was sleeping. She came out of her room and went down the stairs quietly. She looked out the window across the meadow. The grass was moving. There was an early-morning breeze.

She went out of the house and made sure the screen door didn't slam. The breeze felt good on her face. She walked across the yard to the edge of the meadow. She turned to look back and shivered a little. The house was dark and silent in the morning light.

She looked into the tall grass. She stepped forward, pushing the grass

29

apart with her hands, and began to
walk across the meadow. The grass
was wet and cold and some of it hit
her in the face. She walked on think-
ing of the train, the train, the train.

The day was getting brighter. The
sky was turning pink, then orange,
and suddenly the top of the sun came

over the edge of the land, bright,
blinding, to the side of her.

She stopped.

The sun is coming now, she thought.
It seemed friendly to her. Then she
heard odd sounds in the grass. She

froze into stillness. Only her eyes moved. She smiled when she saw them, a family of rabbits rushing through the grass. She stood absolutely still until they had passed. They were only a few feet from her.

She looked back to the house. It seemed a long way away now. So did the fence, but she pushed herself on. She had to push on. She had come this far. She felt a little calmer now, too.

The grass was over her head for a few minutes and she didn't like that, but she pushed it down with her hands. She stopped a moment to

catch her breath, for even though she
had been walking, she felt as if she
had been running very fast.

Now in the silence she heard the
meadow come alive. Now the birds
began chirping a morning song. Were
they greeting her? Were they wel-
coming her to the meadow? There
were more movements in the grass.

The day was beginning for the animals, she thought. Her day had begun long ago, it seemed. The sun was high in the sky. She must hurry on. She was almost to the end of the meadow.

Boom Boom B-boom.

The train was coming.

She ran the rest of the way into the narrow opening between the meadow and the fence where the grass had been cut. She clutched the wire of the fence. It was an open fence, easy to see through. The train was coming.

The track was about twenty feet away but it seemed closer.

The diesel engine came booming down the track. She waved and waved at the engineer. He didn't see her. He was looking down the track. The sound of the wheels and the jerking of the cars surrounded her.

The cars went by. The cattle car and the refrigerator car, the gondola car and the coal car, four automobile carriers, cars loaded with tractors, cars filled with machines she did not recognize. One car was filled with chickens all clucking, another car was for oil, a lot of cars had dirt on them, a lot of cars were closed, rattling noisily by her. Yes, oh yes, she was here. The early-morning train was going by.

She heard the train sound its horn far down the track and the train still

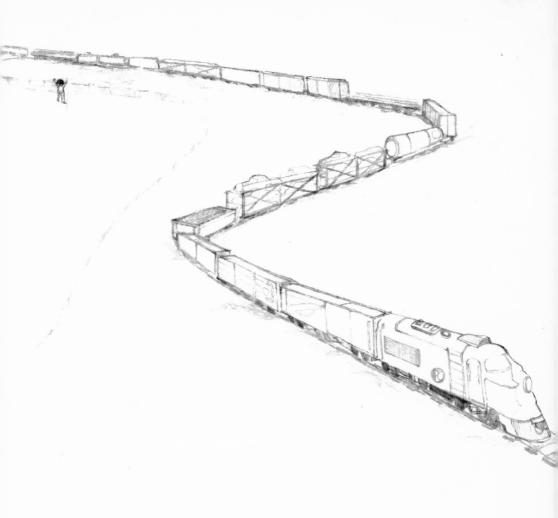

went by her. Her body began to relax
against the fence and she studied the
cars more carefully.

Now she saw the last car, the caboose, and she waved at the man high up in the top of the car. He waved back at her. He was a big man with a beard.

She watched until the train was out of sight and then she laughed. She spread her arms out, and screaming like a hoot owl, she ran across the meadow, spreading the grass away from her as she ran. In no time at all she was home.

She went running into the kitchen. Everyone was at the breakfast table.

"I went to see the trains go by, all by myself," she told them. "And the caboose man waved at me."

"Elizabeth is an adventurer," her father said.

"I told you there was nothing to be afraid of," Tony said.

Georgie smiled at her and her mother put pancakes down in front of her, pancakes with strawberry jam, her favorite breakfast.

She went outside after breakfast and looked across the field. She had gone a long way and come back.

Her mother came to the door and Amy pushed by her mother and came out. Amy took Elizabeth's hand.

"Lizo, me, take me," Amy said. "Take me."

Elizabeth looked at her mother. Her mother shook her head, yes.

"Come back after the noon train for lunch," her mother called after her.

"Maybe we'll see the rabbits, Amy. I saw them this morning. A family of rabbits going by, a mother and a daddy and three little ones."

"I want rabbits," Amy said.

They were disappearing into the tall grass.

"There's nothing to be afraid of, Amy," Elizabeth said.

"I not 'fraid," Amy said.

"Neither am I," Elizabeth said.

The sun was high in the sky now, in a clear blue sky. They walked together across the meadow.

46